A bad boy can be good for a girl

Tanya Lee Stone was an editor of children's books, but when the writing bug hit, she was hooked. Stone holds a degree in English from Oberlin College and a Master's degree in Education. She has published many non-fiction and picture books for children. *A Bad Boy Can Be Good for a Girl* is her first novel. Visit her online at www.tanyastone.com

A BAD BOY CAN BE GOOD FOR A GIRL

TANYA LEE STONE

Quercus

First published in Great Britain in 2008 by
Quercus
21 Bloomsbury Square
London
WC1A 2NS

A CIP catalogue reference for this book is available
from the British Library

ISBN PBO 978 1 84724 461 1

10 9 8 7 6 5 4 3 2 1

Designed and typeset by Rook Books, London
Printed and bound in England by Clays Ltd, St Ives Plc

For Alan, the *best boy* a girl could ever love

JOSIE

FOR THE RECORD

I'm not stuck up.
I'm confident.
There's a big difference.

If I was stuck up
I'd be one of those
'Oh look at me, I'm so pretty'
girls
instead of just appreciating the fact that
my cinnamon skin looks good year-round
and I can hop in the shower after football or lacrosse,
throw on a clean sweatshirt,
sweep on some mascara,
let my hair loose from its pony,
and give any girl
a serious run for her money.

And while I totally deserve my spot in Honours English
I'm happy to take my proper place
in Algebra I, suffering alongside the rest of the
mediocre maths heads.

So,
as far as high-school boys go,
I'm not so floundering in self-esteem issues
that I need
someone's arm to hang on or
someone's jersey number to cheer for
to be a legitimate person,
like some people I know.

Man, to listen to Kim and Caroline
chatter away all summer
you'd think we've been waiting our whole pathetic lives
just to graduate middle school
and get to Point Beach High
so we could date high-school boys.

As if high-school boys
hold some kind of magical key
to who we
all
really
are.

THE WHOLE TRUTH

All that stuff I just said is absolutely
swear-to-God true,
but the rest of the truth
the whole truth
is
lately
I don't have as tight a grip
on my confidence
as usual.
I mean, this is *high school*.
Sure, I was pretty popular in middle school,
but you never know
how these things are going to
turn out.

What if
what Kim and Caroline call
my natural look
is considered totally lame in high school?

What if
wanting to read
during lunch
makes me a
total geek?

What if
I don't
fit in
at
all?

JIGSAW

It's funny how one night can change
the way you look at certain things.

I mean, I believe 100 per cent
that high-school boys don't hold any magical key
or anything
but that's not the same as saying they're all bad.
Some of them aren't so bad.
Like, maybe,
this
one.

I saw him across the gym before he saw me.
He was scoping things out at the Fall Fling,
looking for that one lucky freshman
to win the prize

of dancing
with the studly senior.

I think he picked me
because I looked
right at him
as if I couldn't
care less.

I couldn't care
more.

My heart was pounding,
palms sweaty.
Hit me like a surprise party you cross-your-heart
had no idea
anyone was throwing you.

Now, I have *never* understood all that
he's-my-other-half
soul mate stuff
or when people sometimes talk about
having an empty space inside
or that they're missing pieces or something.

But then
he walked over
and fit himself
right into my puzzle.

FIRST (REAL) DATE: PART ONE

I think Mum is a little bit worried
the first guy I'm dating
is a senior.

She should know me
better than that.
I never do
anything
I don't want to do.
That's not going to change.

I mean, when everyone thought
it was so cool
to sit on the seawall
and puff through a pack of Marlboro Lights,

I had a blast sitting there laughing,
telling them how truly stupid and
uncool
they really were, actually,
coughing and sputtering and wanting to puke,
yeah, *real* sexy,
dopes.
Give me some credit.
I never do
anything
I don't want to do.
Period.

He picks me up in his brand-new
Mazda Miata.

I hate to admit it,
but he kind of cracked my
cool-as-a-cucumber exterior
I tried to pull off
at the dance
(even though I'm hoping
he didn't notice I talked way too fast)

but now
all *he's* talking about
is how many horsepowers his stupid car has
and the torque

and how he almost picked cherry red
but he's so stoked that they had this
sweet ocean colour
come in at the last minute
and I'm starting to think
maybe
I made
a
big
mistake,
but I just smile and nod,
like the idiotic bobblehead
planted
in the middle of his dashboard,
pretending
this is the most
interesting conversation ever.

Man, I hope he doesn't keep this up too long.

We pull in to Smiles.
The parking lot is
alive,
too many radio stations
blaring
kids making out in cars
sitting on hoods
eating hot dogs

high-fiving
smoking various things
drinking various things
talking too loud
about
nothing.

Real fun.

Inside
the scene isn't all that different,
except
it's another kind of dark
punctuated
by the bright lights
of too many pulsing
video games
jammed up
against each other.

We walk over to a big bunch of seniors
by the batting cages
he drapes his arm around me
real possessive,
which should have immediately brought out my
I-can-take-care-of-myself attitude,
but instead stirs this
way-foreign tingly

'Oh my God, he really likes me' rush.
(*Lame! Did I just actually think that?*)

'Dude!'

'Who's the babe? Fresh*meat*?' one of the jocks says,
right in front of my face.

'Get it? Fresh*men*, fresh*meat*?'
He's laughing hysterically,
like this is the most hilarious thing
anyone
has ever
heard.

'Yeah, got it.
Guys, this is Josie.'

A round of Hi's, How's It Goin's, and What's Up's
are tossed in my general direction.

'Hi.'
I never thought this scene
would interest me
but actually,
I feel really,
I don't know,
included, I guess,

with his arm wrapped around me
pulling me into a group –
and not just any group:
the coolest, most popular group of *seniors*,
even though the guys are fairly juvenile.

'Hey, we're all heading over to Lindsey's in a while,'
one of the boys says.
'Time to party!'

'Okay. We'll hit that, too. All right, Jos?'
'Okay. Sure.'

Although I'm not at *all* sure
because my Mum would
freak
if she knew I was going to a
senior party.

FIRST (REAL) DATE: PART TWO

We hang out at Smiles for a while,
eat some truly nasty pizza,
then head over to Lindsey's.

On the drive over
he rests his hand on my thigh,
'Are you having a good time?'

'Yes.'
'Good, I'm glad. I want you to have fun.'

His hand
is still
on my
thigh.

He's going on and on about something,
his car again, I think,
but I can't concentrate
with his fingers moving back and forth like that
and even though he's acting real
innocent,
like he's got no *goal* or anything,
the heat from his fingers is
searing through to my skin
like one of those iron-on transfers.
I could almost bet
when I look later
his handprint
will have been permanently
imprinted
on my leg.

Then he raises the stakes.
He moves his hand onto mine
picks it up
and puts it on
his thigh.

He takes his eyes off the road
for a second
looks at me
and smiles.

Like the big bad wolf.

If I was in a comic strip,
there'd be a bubble coming out of my head
with the word 'Gulp' in it.

FIRST (REAL) DATE: PART THREE

We did *not* have parties
like this
in middle school.

Kids are doing, I'm not even sure what,
in rooms that aren't
really part of the party.

Lindsey lives in Morningside
along the shoreline
where the seawall is made of giant slabs
of granite and quartz.
Some are slippery smooth and catch the moonlight.
Some are rough with little crags and crevices
perfect for

wedging
the toe or heel of a sneaker in to keep from slipping
down the wall.
I spot couples
sprawled out in different spots
on the huge quilt made of stone.
Her parents must be
way out of town.

'Cool party, huh?' he says.
'Uh, yeah.'

Apparently, I wasn't convincing.

'Relax, Josie, people are just having fun.
You're a big girl now,' he says.

'Gee, thanks for telling me,
otherwise I wouldn't have known,' I say.
(Who the hell does this guy think he is?!)

'Oh, don't be that way. I'm sorry.
I didn't mean anything by it. Dance?'

We move onto the dance floor,
if you can call a living room with all the furniture
pushed up against one wall
and plastic cups tipping stale beer

all over the place
a dance floor.
With every step
my shoes stick a little to the
spilled drinks coating the wood like slightly used tape.

A lot of boys don't dance,
they're too cool.
Not this one.
He's *way* too interested in getting his body
up against mine.

As he pulls me into him,
full contact,
I feel like my brain's going to explode
from all the fighting going on inside it.
I mean, this is the kind of guy
Caroline would fall for,
not *me*.
I'd be the one to point out to her later
that this was the exact moment
she should have gotten the message
and walked.
But instead
I smile
wrap my arms around his neck
and sink into his chest.
Damn.

Why does he have to
smell
so . . . so . . .
Yum.

Now we're basically just hugging to the music,
as opposed to *actual* dancing
and as he starts kissing me
I realize
I better get home
before things get out of hand
on our first (real) date.

FALLING

This boy is slick.
For a few weeks now I've felt like part of me
is watching
a really stupid 'teen' movie
thinking,
I can't believe he actually said that!
while the other part of me is
totally soaking it up.

Like when he told me I was so gorgeous
I could wear a burlap sack
and still be better looking than
any other girl in my class.

I hate to admit this,
but I think my actual response was to giggle and blush.

Or when he was waiting for me
at the main entrance one morning
and kissed me for five minutes
in front of the entire school.

I can't help it.
There's just something about him.

Like the way he seems so super confident
about sex,
always saying how good he wants to make me feel
and how his older brother (who's in college)
told him all about how to make a girl really happy
in bed,
and when was I going to let him show me.

So of course I'm wondering what he means by that,
it's a turn-on because he's got me really curious,
but really nervous at the same time,
and I keep hearing that expression in my head
'like a moth to a flame'
and wondering if that's what it means
as I feel myself
totally

out-of-control
falling
for
him.

HOME

How can I feel
so completely
connected
to someone
I practically just met?

Where did this
Oh! There he is!
feeling come from?

He smiles at me
and I'm home.

He touches me
and I'm home.

He kisses me
and I'm home.

BOOSTER SHOT

It's not just how he makes me feel
that's so different.

I mean, I've always been considered pretty cool,
but this is high school,
so my coolness factor was pretty much up for grabs
the second I entered the building.

When I'm walking down the hall with him,
everybody knows I'm somebody.

Kim and Caroline are puffed up by it too.
We're the freshmeat girls.

Not loving that name,
but I'll let it slide for now.

THE DEEP END

After school
if the swim team isn't using it
the pool is open to anyone.

We could just go down to the beach I guess,
but it's a little too chilly now
and besides, there aren't any
sharp mussel beds to slice your feet on here.

Swimming was his idea.
He has half an hour to kill before football practice.

I've spent half my life
messing around with my friends
in the Sound.

But playing in the water with them
was never like this.

First of all, I'm extremely aware
that I'm practically half-naked
even though I did pick out this ratty old one-piece
instead of a
make-his-tongue-hang-out bikini.
I was trying not to send any mixed messages –
but he's still looking at me like he wants to
eat me alive.

He says things like 'You're so soft, you feel so good,'
lame things
that shouldn't work on anybody
but actually work on everybody.

I'm concentrating more on
dodging his hands
than swimming,
since I don't think there's a spot on me
he hasn't grazed
in the name of good old-fashioned water-play.

He pulls a dolphin move,
popping up again near the diving board.
'C'mere, babe. There's no one around.
Come get me in the deep end.'

I shake my head and climb out
on the edge,
sticking only the tips of my toes
in the water.
That's as far as I'm going
today.

PUSHING MY LUCK

I said I didn't want to
cut class
but he was whispering in my ear,
chipping away at
my common sense.
'Yeah you do, honey.
You *really* do.
We'll have a blast. I *promise*.'

Down the hall
around the corner
through the doors
and out.

We're OUT!

We run behind this gargantuan oak tree
ducking out of sight.
He lifts my whole entire body right up in the air
slides me down him
pulls me in
kisses me hard
we stumble to the ground.

But as I fall
I hear a voice rise from deep inside,
hurtle closer, faster,
then slam into my ears,
'What are you *doing*?
This isn't you.'

I untangle myself from his arms,
and run.

I reach the doors
as the bell rings,
slipping into the seat
that is expecting me.

Safe.

But the knot in my stomach
betrays me
to me.

I know
I'm
pushing my luck.

NO-MAN'S-LAND

High school has its own terrain.
When you're in class,
you're in class.
You know where you're supposed to sit.

But when there's free time,
it's harder to know who's supposed to go where.

The caf is the trickiest minefield to manoeuvre.
Especially when you're a freshman.
The cool kids usually take up the centre
and various groups line the edges.
Freshmen need to figure out where they fit in fast,
before people claim spots.
Once that happens, you're pretty much

stuck where you are,
or left out completely,
so you'd better choose well.

Kim, Caroline, and I had a plan.
We would stick together –
under no circumstances would we let any of the team
fend for herself
and end up stranded in no-man's-land.

But when he came over to our table
and leaned in to kiss me
and asked me to join him for lunch,
it was really, really, really, really hard
to say
No.

But I did.
No soldier left behind, right?
Or is it: All's fair in love and war?
I can't remember.

ALL'S FAIR IN LOVE AND WAR

Yeah, that's what I'm going with.
I mean, Kim and Caroline
should understand.
Shouldn't they?
When a hot guy invites you to lunch,
you go, right?

Well, I did.
The very next day.
Left them sitting there.

And I was friendly,
it's not like anyone snubbed them.
We walked past their table to say Hi
and even waved a couple of times during lunch.

They didn't wave back.

And they didn't seem to care
when I told them he said,
'Your friends are hot.'

I'll catch up with them later.

I'm sure it will be
fine.

HOT WATER

My parents back out of the driveway.
I peek into my little sister's room – sound asleep.
The knock I'm waiting to hear hits the front door.

He talks me into using the hot tub.
He didn't bring a suit so he says it's not fair
if he's the only one without one.
He says it's dark out anyway,
and he won't look while I get in.
Yeah, like I believe that.

I have actually never used my parents' hot tub.
I didn't think I would like to be in such
hot water
but now that I am,

slippery seal bodies
winding around each other,
I guess I do.

At least the I
who I am
when I'm with him
does.

He pulls me close and kisses me,
then he's kissing my neck and I'm kissing his,
wet and salty,
trying so hard to concentrate only on
how *his* hands feel.

I'm way too scared to touch him down there
but it does feel good
to let him
touch me.
Still, I'm definitely not ready to go
underwater exploring
to see what he has in store for me.
I'm sticking to playing with his gorgeous blond hair
and running my hands all over his
chest
and arms
and back.

This is nice, I'm fine,
I'll just let his fingers wander where they like,
the water's warm and
his hands feel
really, really good,
even though they're going places
no one else's hands but mine have ever gone.

I'm getting really hot,
like I might even pass out,
and I'm not sure if it's the steaming tub
or him
that's making my heart race like this.

His kisses are long
and he's holding me
and touching me
and I'm starting to wonder
what I want
to do
next.

THE PLUNGE

We're in his car.
Let's face it,
there's only one reason to be here –
total privacy.

Most of me wants to be here,
part of me doesn't.
That part turns out to be big enough
to keep stopping him
from unbuttoning my jeans,
pushing away fumbling fingers,
redirecting them under my sweater.

He is
not
satisfied.

'Baby, *please*, don't make me wait any more.
I don't think I can stand it.
It's not like we haven't seen each other naked.
What are you afraid of . . . ?'

Maybe I should just close my eyes and jump in
Fast.
Like ripping off a Band-Aid
with a smiling scream.
Like shooting down the waterslide face-first,
slipping and sliding until . . .

No.

Even though he says things like
'I've never met anyone like you' and
'I could really fall for you.'

It's still
No.

Not
yet.

TWO WORDS

Phone rings.
'It's me.'

A code.
As if to say,
Who else could it be?
he claims me with
a two-word combination
to my personal lock.

WHITE-HOT

I think his smile must give off all the heat
I'll ever need.
It's hot
like a branding iron

and sweet.

Delicious.

As the weather gets colder
it pulls me in,
his warm cosy fire
growing hotter by the minute, hour, day, week,

I may just spontaneously combust
right here
in his arms.

FAVOURITE THINGS

My aunt is over and she's asking me what my favourite
things are. Mine are all so boring, but I can tell you
all his favourite things. He likes greasy cheeseburgers
from Paul's, NASCAR races, playing football with his
brothers, taking me to Showcase Cinemas and not
watching the movie, playing with my necklace when
he talks to me, watching me walk to class . . .

What was the question again?

Oh, right, my favourite things.

I try hard to concentrate
because she's getting this irritated
I-can't-believe-you're-turning-into-one-of-*those*-girls
look on her face.

It's coming back to me . . .
My favourite things?
Uh, let's see, fresh clam pizza from Pepe's;
my musty blue rabbit's foot with one toenail too long;
that photo of the old Chevy completely covered in
all kinds of weird buttons;
the big yellowish boulder in the middle of the jetty
that's the only thing left sticking up at high tide – like
a whale's back, which is why I call it Moby Dick;
that gasp of air you take after popping up from
underneath a huge wave;
a hermit crab scurrying across my foot underwater;
the smack of a puck landing in my hand at my first

(no, wait, that one's not mine –
but man, you should see how good he looks
in his jersey).

I'm sorry,
what was the question again?

SLAMMED

My back is up against his locker,
the knob poking me.
He presses into my body
leaning in tight to share a secret
saved for my ears alone.

I barely hear his words,
too dizzy from his lips
on my earlobe,
too distracted by the smell of him
to listen.

His muffled laugh sends
a puff of warm breath
to caress my cheek.

Then BAM!
He takes
two
giant
steps
back
as his too-cool-for-school buddies
come out of nowhere.

Bright blue eyes go dull;
I'm left with an
I-couldn't-care-less face.
Like I'm not even there.

'Later, Jos.'
He's gone.

What was that?

I blink fast to keep the tears from coming,
but some slip through.
I wipe my eyes with the back of my hand –
black mascara streaks
matching my black mood.

IN AND OUT

I'm sitting on Moby Dick
thinking about everything that's happened
and it's only been
a few weeks.

The tide's coming in,
the smaller rocks I use
to climb up on Moby
already covered over.

I could sit here until the tide comes
all the way in
and goes back out again
for all he'd care.

Seems like five minutes ago
I was the 'only one' he could talk to
the 'only one' he felt comfortable with
the 'only one' who let him be himself
the 'only one' he told stuff to
even stuff you don't tell just anyone.
Like the time his dad caught his Mmum
having dinner with a 'business associate'
when she said she was going shopping with the girls,
and how pissed he was that his dad just stood there,
couldn't believe what a wimp the Old Man was being.
He said that would never happen to him
and clenched his jaw
when he said it.
And even though he didn't say more,
I didn't push it.
I just listened.

And now . . . nothing.

First I'm in
then I'm out.
I just don't get this
hot and cold
thing.

Why does he act like such a jerk

every time it seems like we
get a little bit closer?

And why do I eat it up
later
when he graces me with his presence
and that smile that
looks like
it's just
for
me?

It shouldn't make everything okay.

So
why
does
it?

TESTING THE WATERS

It's too cold for swimming
so he tosses a blanket
a six-pack
and some crisps and salsa
into the dinghy.
We head out
to his parents' boat.

It's anchored pretty close to shore
so it only takes a couple of minutes to reach it.
When you live a few houses from the water
you can tie up pretty much anywhere.

He climbs on first,
reaching his hand down
to help pull me up.

He opens two beers and hands me one.
'Corrupting a minor?' I say, only half joking.
I take a long swig to settle my nerves.

We're totally alone
and I'm not sure how much longer
I'm going to be able to hold out on him.
According to him, he's been *unbelievably ultra*patient.
Plus, I really do have the all-out
hots for him.

He grins.
I think
I'm in trouble.

I've got that tingly sensation again,
the kind where your body is *awake*
and you're not so sure if that's a good thing
or a bad thing.

He spreads the blanket
on the deck
we stretch out
under the stars,
literally.

The sky is amazing tonight.

He tries to point out Cassiopeia
all nonchalant and seafaring-like.
I laugh, forgetting for a split second
how stark raving terrified I am.

'You're *so* way off.
Cassiopeia is over *there*.'
I move his hand so his finger points to the right spot.

'Oh, yeah?
Let's see what you really know,'
rolling over in one smooth move
so that he's pretty much lying
on top of me.

Shark attack.

ROCKING THE BOAT

We kiss for what seems like
forever,
which is a smart move on his part,
because now
I'm actually *wanting* him
to try something
else.

I move my body against his,
raising myself up off the deck
to get
a little closer.

He picks up on that signal
like he's just tuned in to the station
he was looking for.

'God, Josie, you feel so good.'
'Mmm, you too.'

He unzips my sweatshirt jacket
touching my breasts
lightly with his fingertips.

I shiver.

'Are you cold?' he says.
'No.'
'Let me warm you up.'

His mouth is warm and wet on my skin,
kissing my mouth, chin, ears, neck
burying his face between my breasts
cold night air brushing against skin
sending tremors through me
his mouth devours me
moving back up to my
neck, ears,
mouth,
never stopping too long in any one spot

until I'm squirming
like crazy.

'Tell me what you want,' he says.
'I don't know, don't stop.'

His hands slide down my stomach
fingers pop open the top snap of my jeans
then unzip.

'Lift up your hips,' he says.
I do what I'm told.

He tugs my jeans down
I feel his breath on me.

I moan.

I open my eyes for a second
and catch him looking at me
like he's waiting for me to give him
the go-ahead.

We lock eyes.
He grins.
I close my eyes again
and moan.

I'm drowning in him.

My hands wander
through his hair
over his back. . . .

He moans.

He rolls off me for a second,
I hear the crackle of a wrapper tearing open
then a zipper,
he rolls back
bare legs against mine.

He kisses me again
deeper this time
his tongue probing
we rock against each other
matching the rhythm
of the water rocking the boat
slapping against its sides in beat
with our bodies.

'Josie, please, I've waited . . .'

His fingers slide my underwear down
I feel him hard against my leg

cross my fingers, hope to die, swear on the Bible,
I
can't
breathe.

In one more second it will be too late.

'WAIT!'

COLD FRONT

We get dressed
in silence
(except I hear him swearing
under his breath).

We row back to shore
in silence.

The only sound
our oars
dipping into dark water
our shoes
crunching snail and mussel shells
sand and rocks
on the way up the beach.

He doesn't look at me once
on the drive home.

I pull my jacket tighter around me.

He pulls into my driveway.

'I'm sorry,' I say.

'It's okay.
See you at school,' he says.

He backs out of the driveway
before I'm even in the door.

SUNK

I wasn't supposed to be there.
I was supposed to be in study hall,
but I got out with a lavatory pass
and a chance to see him
so I could explain.

I wasn't supposed to hear.

'What are you putting *up* with that chick for, man?'
one of his
thick-necked, detention-duty, jerkoff
jock friends says.
'You haven't even nailed her yet!'

   'I'll get her to come around, I've just gotta work
a little harder on this one,' he says.

'You're nuts, man, you've worked hard *enough*.
Time to move on.
Even if she does look like Ashley,'
his idiot friend of fresh*meat* fame says.

I see his face go hard, jaw clenched like before.
Who's Ashley?

'Yeah, well, I almost did her the other night, then she
freaked. Josie's hot and all, but the whole thing is
getting pretty old,' he says.

I feel sick.
Tumbling,
head-pounding,
veins
in
the
back
of
my
neck throbbing,
heart-racing
sick.

I used to be so strong.

I mean, for crying out loud,

when our cat got hit by a car
and my parents weren't home
and my little sister was hysterical
I was the one who wrapped Sweet Pea
in a towel
and called the vet
and called my parents
and comforted my sister.
And that was a dead cat!

Could it really be this easy
for a guy
to make me
weak?

I run back to study hall before he sees me.

We didn't speak all weekend.
He never called,
and even though I
really
wanted to,
I didn't let myself
call him.

MISERABLE

Him:
'You're taking this way too seriously, Jos.
It just didn't work out.
We want different things, that's all.'

Me:
'I thought you cared about me.'

Him:
'You know I do.'

Me:
'Clearly, I don't know squat.'

OFF

It's over.

How can a person,
any person,
even just a friend,
turn off,
snap –
just
like
that?

Lights out, nobody's home.
Like he never even knew me.

How stupid was I

to think he cared about me,
or even thought of me
as a real, live, feeling
person, even?

Please, God, don't let
most boys be like this.

I'll have to become a
nun
or a
gym teacher
or
something.

KIM AND CAROLINE

'Oh, so, *suddenly*
we're your best friends again?'
Caroline wants to know.
Kim's nodding like always.

'Where were you when we
needed to talk?' Caroline says.
Kim nods.

'I mean, we promised to stick together
and you run off with Mr Wonderful
and leave us in the dust!'

I guess they're pretty mad at me.

'He's not so wonderful any more, is he?'
Caroline's pleased with herself.
She sure told me.

She's right, of course.
I have no excuse.
None.
I *did* leave them in the dust.
And for what?

I try to tell them
but the words get all caught up
in trying to explain what happened
with him
and I bawl.
Really,
all-and-all-out
bawl.

Caroline puts her arm around me.
'Don't cry, Josie,
it'll be okay,' she says.
Kim nods.

NEXT TIME

I hope
next time
(because, unfortunately, you *know* there's going to be
a next time),
I'll be smarter.
Oh God, please let me *act*
as smart as
I *am*.

I'll try to remember to look for the signs.
You know, the ones that point to maybe a guy honing
in on you for reasons other than you're a decent-
looking member of the opposite
sex.

The signs that maybe, just maybe,
he might actually like you
for
YOU.

I'm going to look for a boy
who will look at me and
at least
try
to see me.

Me.

Not a girl,
not a hot girl,
not a brainy girl,
not a funny girl,
not a dark girl,
not a pretty girl,

ME.

FOREVER

I hope I remember these feelings
forever

stupid
humiliated
foolish
stung
heartbroken
pissed off
and a little
bit
wiser.

I want to remember
forever,

so I never fall for this kind of boy
again.

It would be nice
if there was some manual
some little book where a girl could look up
what to do
what not to do
and who not to do it with.

The truth is, I want to remember the good parts
forever
too,
head spinning
mood lifting
confidence boosting
insides quivering
legs going weak
heart going crazy
body letting loose.

The whole thing reminds me
of this girl Katherine
I read about in middle school
in a book called
Forever.

I remember *exactly* how Katherine felt
having all this love and sex stuff happen
for the first time and

even though they didn't end up together
forever
like she thought they would
she knew she'd remember that
grab-at-your-heart
blinding
he's-my-whole-world
nothing-else-matters-but-him
feeling
forever.

Of course, in the actual *Forever*,
the boy, Michael I think his name was, wasn't a
total jerk
so in real life, my real life,
it's not only the good parts I intend to hold on to
but also how totally
nothing
he made me feel.
I'm hoping that by remembering *that*,
as much as I'd like to forget it,
it'll help keep me from ever
letting a boy
make me feel like
nothing
again.

THE PLAN

What's wrong with boys
like him, anyway?
I mean, he really meant something to me,
but to him
I was just
a girl to 'nail'.
So disgusting.
It makes me want to shake him, shake some sense into
him, hurt him somehow, give him a glimpse of how
totally humiliated and used he made me feel,
penetrate that smug attitude.

That's when it hits me.
I really *should* do something,
warn the others,

so the next girl isn't such an unsuspecting sap.

And I know exactly how.
My weapon of choice:
Forever.

Every girl reads it eventually.
In high school,
or earlier, like me, if they're lucky enough
to hear about it
and there's a copy to nab.
Now every girl,
at least in my school,
will read about
him
at the same time.

Forewarned,
Forearmed.
Forever.

BEWARE

I find what I'm looking for
in the Bs for Blume, Judy.
There's a carrel
where the librarian
can't see me.

I open the book
to the back
where there just happens to be
a bunch of those
blank end pages (are we *supposed* to make notes here?)

I write:

TO THE GIRLS OF POINT BEACH HIGH: BEWARE!!

There's a boy at this school who's only out for
one thing.

I won't stoop to his level and call him by name
but his initials are T. L.
(aka, Two-faced Liar, Terrible Lay
(I'm only guessing), Total Loser)
he's on the football and baseball teams
and he never misses a party.

Sound familiar?

Don't go out with him!
(unless you want to use him for sex
before he uses you)

Forewarned is Forearmed.
Forever.

CHECK IT OUT

It was easy to spread the word.

'Remember that book *Forever*?
Check it out again.
Need-to-know information
has been added
at the back.'

I was on a mission.
Every girl I passed a note to
or whispered to
or told in the cafeteria
nodded like she
got it.

HIGHER EDUCATION

Let's recap, shall we?
I definitely lost some things along the way:

My confidence – a little bit, yeah, but it's coming back.
My better judgement – yep, that definitely went
out the window.
My friends – that was a close one, could have been
a lot worse (although I know they know it's going to
happen to them, which is probably why they cut me
some slack).
My virginity – nope! Still holding on to that!

I found out some things along the way too,
important things.

I didn't cave under pressure (that virginity thing).
And I stood up for myself and fought back,
I'm proud of that.

It's pretty amazing
to find out new things about yourself
when you think you already know every inch
of your own personal landscape.

And it's pretty exciting
to discover that there's probably
a whole lot more to discover
inside this person
that is
me.

It reminds me of the way the sun
hits the water in the afternoon
scattering colour and light
all over the beach
revealing little nooks and crannies
that were always there
but didn't catch my eye until the moment
they sparkled in the sunlight,
impossible to miss.

A lucky feeling floods over me,
washing away pieces of the pain.
Wisdom stings but
ignorance is *not* bliss.

NICOLETTE

POWER PLAY

It didn't take a genius to see it.
All the girls at my school
were always just
waiting.

Waiting
for some guy to call,
waiting
for some guy to say she was
pretty, or
nice, or
smart.

Waiting for some
guy
to make the first move.

Uh-uh. Not me.
Why should I sit around and wait?
It's all about the power.
Who's got it
and who doesn't.

If I say who
and I say when
and I say what
then *I*
have it.
Simple as that.

Let's just leave the rest of the
lovey-dovey crap
out of it,
okay?

I LOVE

the way my body starts to feel
when a boy runs his hands all over me,
first over my clothes,
then getting all under them,
appreciating smooth curves
and hidden places.

I love the way a boy's body feels
when he starts to groan
from my touch,
and he squirms and shifts
and wants me so bad
and tells me so.

and I love, love, love, love
the time when you know
there isn't any place else in the whole wide world
that boy would rather be
than with
you.

That's the power.
When you're the only thing that matters,
the world could come to an end
but the both of you would still be in that happy,
drunk but not drunk,
it should be illegal for a body to feel this good
state of mind.

OF COURSE,

you won't have any power
if people think you're a slut.
And if you're a girl,
and you like to fool around,
you can get a bad rep, fast.

To mess with the rules of the game
you have to know what they are.

That's why I usually hang
with guys
from other schools.

GOOD ENOUGH

But there's this one guy
at my school
I think I'll check out.
This girl named Josie is going around telling everybody
he's no good.
Wanted me to read all about him
in the back of some old library book.
I tell you what, though,
I think she's just a goody-goody.
I have *seen* this guy and he looks pretty good to me.
I mean REAL good.
Finger-*lickin'* good.
She probably just didn't know how to take care of him.
I've *got* his number,
and he's about to get mine.

HEY

I walk straight over to him
as he's digging for stuff in his locker.

'Hey.'
'Hey.'

'Nicolette, right?'
'That's right.'

'Aren't you the girl who used to hang with
Tyler Jones sophomore year?'

For a second I worry how he heard
about me hooking up
with a guy from another school.

But I figure a little mystery can be used to my
advantage.

I fiddle with my top button and give a little sexy smile
like I'm remembering some steamy memory of
me and Tyler.
'Yeaahhh, that's me.'

'How's junior year treating you so far?'
'Can't complain,' I say.

'You and Josie split, huh?' I say.
'You heard about that?'

'Kind of. She told me to stay away from you.'
'But here you are,' he says.
'Here I am.'

He smiles.

I smile back.

'Wanna grab a burger at Paul's later?' he says.
'Okay.'

And that's
how it's done.

BURGER AND SHAKE

'Can I get some fries with that shake?'
He laughs at me with that sexy laugh
as I slink on over to his car with our burgers in a bag.

'So what all happened with you and Josie, anyway?'

'Ah, she's just a kid. No hard feelings,' he says.
'She's not like you, Nic. I've got a feeling you're
all woman.'

He takes that burger right out of my hand and slides
his tongue right in my mouth.

He's kissing me so good
I'm hoping he doesn't try much else

because sometimes
to make things go
the way you want
you need to know when
to take it
slow.

FINE

Dad's been gone since
I was five,
but we're fine,
Mum and me.
We look out for each other.
Sure, she spends a lot of time
on the dating scene, but that has its perks.
I have the freedom I need,
access to tons of hot clothes –
we're about the same size, and she's got good taste.
Some people say she dresses too young for her age,
but she's got a great body and she's proud of it.
Why shouldn't she be?
She taught me to be proud too.
Powerful and proud,

that's how Mum says a woman's got to be
to get what she wants
out of this world.

NICOLETTE

I've always liked my name.
It's different and kind of sexy.
But it's never sounded half as sexy
as when it's *his* voice
saying it over and over and over and over
right in my ear
as his fingers tangle through
my thick blonde hair
and his hands travel around
my back
my neck
my belly
my boobs.

Nicolette. Ohh, Nicolette.

Nicolette, you're so soft.
Nicolette, you feel so good.
Nicolette.

AFTER PRACTICE

I'm waiting for him
like he asked,
which I'm sort of kicking myself for.
I should be making him wait for me,
not the other way around.

But here he comes
running off the field
over to me.
He's got my full attention.
Can't seem to help myself.

'Hey, you,' he says.
'Hey.'

'You look great,' he adds.

My 'thanks'
cut off
by his mouth on mine.
Overpowered
by the force of his kiss
bulk of his uniform
smell of his sweat.
Hands everywhere.

Then,

'Thanks, babe,
gotta get home for dinner!'
and he sprints towards the gym
before
I can
say
anything,
like,
'Hey,
I thought we had
plans!'

RED LIGHT

There's an old art supply closet at the end of
Yellow Hall.
I never knew it was there until he showed it to me
the other day.
It's got this red lightbulb in the ceiling because it used
to be a darkroom or something.
He says it's our very own red-light district,
whatever that means.
I like that we have a place all our own.
He put a piece of dark tape over the outside switch,
that way nobody can tell when the red light's lit.
None of the teachers or janitors seem to notice, or care.
There are shelves with leftover art supplies,
like paint and brushes.

It smells good in there,
like potential,
like anything
is just waiting to be made
into something.

GREEN LIGHT

Here he comes, looking right at me with that grin.
But he doesn't say anything, just shoves
a note in my hand and
brushes on past.

'Isn't that the girl you were telling us about?'
one of his friends says.
I hear him say, 'Yeah, that's her,'
and I'm caught off guard by my insides jumping
at the thought of him
talking to his friends about me.

Could he really like me,
for real?
And could I

really like him,
too?

I open my palm.

RLD: 10:15

At 10:10, I change to Green and GO.

THE CLOSET

I open the door and slip inside,
he's not here yet, oh great,
I wish I hadn't shown up first.

Too late.

Here he is.
'How much time do you have?'
'Only a few minutes, I've gotta get to my next class,'
I say.
'Well, I've gotta get to you.
I've been thinking about you all morning,' he says.

My body's pulsing and my cheeks are probably flushing,
I'm glad our red light is hiding that.

'C'mere.'
He holds me against him and kisses me,
Omigod I love how he kisses me,
a little bit forceful but gentle at the same time.
Each kiss
hotter and wetter
our bodies pressing closer and closer
his jeans stretched tight against his hard-on.
I'm getting that tingle down low
my body wanting him more and more and more
my head trying to keep it together.

Just as I'm finding the strength to stop,
he reaches down to my trousers
spreads his palm open
presses his fingers against me.
'Nic, you're so . . .'
his words crumble into a moan.

Now I'm *needing* him
but I still don't want him to feel
how much.

Too late.

His hand disappears into my pants.

I'm so hot for him,

too hot, really.

I can feel my
I say who and
I say what
slipping.

Who's got the power now?
Is it still me?

My chest feels warm
almost
burning.

It's me,
losing
control.

Losing
my
cool.

The bell rings.

He whips his hand out,
looks me dead in the eye and says,
'Gonna be late for English. Catch ya later, Nic.'
And he leaves.

Just like that.

And now, I'm gonna be late too.

I straighten my clothes,
take a deep breath,
and get my ass to class.

WE HAD

the same lunch period today.
I thought it might be nice to sit with him,
but when I looked for a seat
there was no room anywhere at his table
and he never caught my eye.

I don't know how he didn't see me,
I walked pretty near his table.
I thought it was obvious I was looking for a seat,
but I guess he didn't see me.

POWER OUTAGE

It's been two days since those mind-blowing minutes
in our closet.
In bed at night
my hands retrace
every move his hands
made.

Why hasn't he called me,
or found me in school to say something – *anything*?
Is he *trying* to make me crazy?

I can't believe it,
but for once, I actually *want* a guy
to pay more attention to me,
take me out,

show me off,
meet his friends,
even some of the girls,
since most of the ones at PBH
don't give me the time of day.
I think they think I'm a threat or something,
even though I hardly ever go after their guys.

I wouldn't mind him
treating me like his
girlfriend.

I don't think I'm playing
any more.

It never occurred to me I couldn't change
the way things are
whenever I wanted to.
I mean, I've always
been the one
calling the shots.

I saw him a few times in the halls
and he winked at me,
but we never seem to get a chance to talk.

I was starting to wonder if I was imagining
what was happening

between us
when his car pulls up next to me
about a block from school
and he asks if I want a ride home.

I let my breath out.

I didn't even realize I was holding it.

I climb in and flash my sexiest smile.

'How are you? I've been missing you,'
trying to sound casual,
but wishing right away I could take it back.

'Oh yeah?' he says.
He looks at me.
'Me too.
There's something special about you, Nic,' he adds.

Mmmmmm.

THE LONG WAY HOME

'I know a place where we can stop
on the way home,' he says.

'Okay, and then we can study together at my house.'
'Okay.'

We pull onto Fowler Field and he stops the car.
'Let's go for a walk.'

We walk toward the baseball diamond,
then right into the empty dugout.

'What's here?'
'Us,' he says.

We sit on the bench.

'You know I really like you, right?' he says.

What I'm thinking is,
Thank God he said it first.

What I say is,
'Sure, I get that.'

'So, will you do something for me?'
He starts unzipping his jeans.
'I promise to return the favour,' he says.

And there he is, in broad daylight,
standing right in front of me
jeans around his ankles.
Guys.
Not a bashful bone in their bodies.
Why can't we be like that?

'I think we're going too fast,
I mean, we haven't even gone out on a date yet,'
I hear myself say.
(*I can't remember the last time I used the word* date.)

'We will, Nic, I promise. But we're here now,
and I'm dying for you. *Please*, baby.'

I put my mouth on him
and he groans,
making me want
to please him
even more.
I know how
to take him
over
the
edge.

'Now it's your turn,' he says.

Most guys don't think about what the girl's getting,
they're just out for themselves.

He pulls me to my feet and turns me around
so he's standing in back of me.
'C'mere.'

It's chilly enough to see our breath.
I should be
shivering
but he's wrapped himself around me
strong body
and hands
warming me all over.

He turns me around again so I'm facing him,
unzips my trousers
eases them down over my hips
and kisses me,
gently guiding me back down
to the bench.

Then his mouth leaves mine.

The back of me
stings
from the cold dugout against my skin,
the front of me
steams
from his touch.

I'm
buzzing.
My eyes are open
but things
aren't
quite
in
focus.

His hair so soft through my fingers,
I close my eyes and my head falls back
against the wall.

My heart
might actually pound
right out of my chest.

I couldn't move myself from this spot
if the dugout caught fire.

On the way home,
head on his shoulder, his
'you're the best'
whispers down
reaching a spot
in my soul.

I didn't realize until later that night
that he never came in to study
when he dropped me off.

FAVOUR

Phone rings.
It's him.

'Do me a favour?'
'Another one?'

He laughs.
'Wear a skirt tomorrow.'

'Why?'
' 'Cause.'

' 'Cause why?'
'You'll see.'

I couldn't help it.
I thought about him
all night.

SECOND THOUGHTS

When I find the note on my locker:

RLD: Study Hall

I have second thoughts.
He *had* to have seen me in the cafeteria
this time.
Either that, or he's blind
or he doesn't think I'll like his friends,
or that they'll like me.

I decide to go
just so I can find out
what his deal is.

He's waiting for me when I get there.

He looks at my clothes and grins.

'I just happened to want to wear a skirt today.'

'And what a lovely skirt it is.'

'How come you didn't invite me over at lunch?'

There, I said it. But I'd also just left myself
wide open.

Instinct kicks in,
I fold my arms across my chest quick.
What was I thinking,
letting some guy get to me like this?

'What are you talking about?' he says.

'Every time I see you at lunch
you won't look at me.
What's the matter, I'm not good enough
for your friends?'

'Nic, I don't know *what* you're talking about.
I just didn't see you.

I swear.'

I so
want
to believe him.

I uncross my arms.
'Really?'
'Of course, honey. What kind of a jerk do you think
I am?
C'mere.'

The 'honey' got me.

And now he's
kissing me slow
touching me sweet
sliding my skirt up
making me
want
him
all over
again.

'Nice skirt. Easy access. A little tip I picked up
from my big brother.'
'Smart brother.'

'You still mad at me?'
I manage an 'Uh-uh.'

'Good. I'm taking you on a date tomorrow.'

One more wet kiss
and off he goes.

PIZZA AND BEER

'Wanna get some pizza later?'

'Is this that real date you promised?'

'Yeah.'

'Pizza's not much of a date.'
'It's what I'm in the mood for, that's all.'

'Okay, but come by my house and pick me up.
You can meet my mum.'

At 6:45 he honks his horn.
'Come on in and say hello,' I yell from the window.

'Nah, I'm hungry, let's go!'

I grab my bag and slide into the seat next to him.

'Mmm, you look good enough to eat,' he says.
'Maybe we should skip the pizza.'
'No, c'mon, I'm hungry too, take me OUT.'
I toss my head back, shaking my hair.
I *know* I look good.

I'll make this boy so proud to be seen with me
and so happy
he won't know what hit him.

Twenty minutes later I'm sitting on his lap,
steering wheel moulded into my back,
feeding him a slice.
I lick the sauce from around his lips.
He tips a beer bottle into my mouth,
lapping up what spills down my chin with his tongue.

He starts unbuttoning my top,
one button, then two, three, four.

Fixing his eyes on mine and smiling that smile,
he cups my boobs in both hands
and squeezes them
rubbing his thumbs back and forth against my nipples,

sending lightning bolts through my body.

He pulls my bra off to the side
leaning his head into my chest.
I want him to swallow me whole.

We're both warm and sweaty.
I'm dizzy.
The heat from his jeans is rising
right through my skirt.

He reaches down to slide the seat back
giving us more room
unzips his jeans
and out it springs,
like an animal that's been waiting to be let out,
which is pretty much true.

I suck my breath in fast
as he slips on a condom.
Then his hands are on my thighs, under my skirt,
my whole body is unfolding to him,
I lift my hips up – 'Yes,' he whispers.

I can feel him move through me
all the way up to the top of my head
and all the way down to the soles of my feet
as we melt into each other

over and over and over
until I think I'm hollering
and he's yelling
'Yes, Yes, Yes, YES!'
I collapse into his shoulders
and everything goes quiet.

I've never felt happier in my whole life.

So this is what love feels like.

CLOSE ENCOUNTER

Blue Hall is crammed with people:
The Lunch Hour rush.
I'm trying to grab some stuff from my locker.
There's a hand on my butt.
Hey!
It better be him, or somebody's getting slugged.
It is him.
He's never touched me in front of other people before.
'Cut it out,' I tease.
'Nobody can see anything in this traffic jam,
chill out,' he says, with a little edge in his voice
I haven't heard before.
Then he locks his eyes on mine
reaches down
and touches me right *there*. I can't breathe.

'Meet me at Red Light.'
And he's swallowed up into the crowd.

NEW FRIENDS

I'm walking to Red Light and I see a group
of his friends walking towards me.
I'm not sure if
I should say anything,
because we've never
been introduced.

'Hi, Nicolette,' one guy says.
'Hey, Nic.' Another tosses his chin my way.
The girls look in the opposite direction.

'Hey, guys!' I say, probably a little too enthusiastically,
but c'mon, I'm trying to make an effort here.

The boys grin at each other as they all keep walking.

NEW ENEMIES

Before I get to our place
here come some more.
Just girls this time.

These are the picture-perfect girls
who only go out with jocks,
they probably don't like that I'm taking
one of their own.
As if they could get him.
They wouldn't know what to do with him.
He's probably already worked his way through them
and figured that out,
which is why
he's
with
me.

I'm thinking all of this when they walk by
and one of them says to the other, like I'm not
even there, like I can't even hear them, like I'm not
even a person,

'Can you believe he's wasting his time with *her*?
She must be as trashy as she looks
to keep him coming back for more.'

If she hadn't already moved on a few yards down the hall
I'm not sure I could have stopped myself from
slapping her.

I spin in their direction and yell.
'Trashy! I'm not trashy, I'm a
woman, unlike you little girls.
If you want a guy like him, you'll have to get a clue.'

They laugh to each other, all superior. One says,
'You're the one who needs to get a clue.
I mean, *hello*, Red Light? Are you *that* stupid
you don't even know when
someone's calling you
a whore?'

ALL BETTER

I make it to our closet and hope he got there first.
He did, he's waiting.
'Nic.' He pulls me in and starts kissing my face, my
ears, my neck, my chest . . .

I push him away.
'Stop it, LOOK at me, can't you see I'm a mess!'
I've got to tell him how they hurt me, but
this is so not cool, and not sexy.
I'm blubbering like a baby.

I repeat the whole nasty thing anyway, word for word,
leaving out the whore part.
He smooths my hair away from my face,
wipes my tears, so tender.

He really does care.

'Don't cry, baby. They're just jealous. Don't waste your time thinking about them. C'mere, baby, let me make you feel all better. . . .'

AVIVA

'WHO the HELL is Aviva?'
I walk right up to his locker
parting the circle of jocks.

'Don't make a scene, Nic,' he says.
Some of his friends laugh.
'Are you laughing at ME?'
My words fly out like so much spit.
'Good luck, man.' And they walk.

'What's the big deal?' he says.

'What's the big DEAL?'

'We never said we couldn't see other people.

I thought we were just having fun.'

I'd be lying
if I said I couldn't believe what I was hearing,
It's not like I'd never heard it before,
but it still felt like someone just
knocked the wind out of me.

'Oh, we were having a lot more than FUN and you
KNOW it! I thought you cared about me. But you
were just playing me the whole time, WEREN'T
YOU?'

'C'mon, Nic. You know you wanted it as much as I did.
You're a blast, but let's face it,
we were just messing around.
It's not like we ever *really* went out.
I never even met your mum.'

'YOU WOULD NEVER COME IN!'

'Nic, I'm sorry, really, I am,
I didn't mean for you to get hurt.
Of course I care about you. I just took her to a party,
it's no big deal.'

'It IS a big deal. You never even THOUGHT
about taking me to a party, did you,

introducing me to your friends.
I wasn't good enough, right?
But Aviva, you asked.
Aviva, what kind of a stupid name is that, anyway?
Josie told me you were no good. She got that right.
I should have listened to her.'

I turn to leave.
As soon as my back's to him,
the tears slip out of my eyes
and run down my cheeks,
but they just keep falling
because there is no way
I'm going to let him
see me
wipe
them
away.

FADE TO BLUE

I run.
I want to get as far away
from him
as fast
as I can.
Far away from the almighty jock-filled Orange Hall.

I run and run
tripping down the stairs,
bursting through the doors to Blue Hall,
racing to my locker to grab my stuff.

I can see the patch of white halfway down the hall:
another note.
I get my things, slam the door, and crumple the paper.

I'm so outta here.
If I was never anyone's girlfriend
I'm not going to read some stupid note so I can be
dumped in writing
by some boy who never came close
to being a boyfriend.

DOG

I don't even have a dog to curl up with, to drown my tears into his shaggy fur. Not even a damn dog around to help me get over the human dog-faced piece of crap I just gave my whole heart and soul and body to. Mum says it's hard enough to take care of ourselves, let alone have time for any mangy mutt. But even a mangy mutt might help me believe I've got some kind of friend in this world.

NO MORE TEARS

I don't think there's a drop of salty water left
in my whole body.

I cried walking home, I cried trying to fit my key into
the front door, I cried climbing the steps to my
bedroom, I cried looking in the mirror at my pathetic
self, I cried pulling off my 'trashy' clothes, and I cried in
the shower. I cried so hard in the shower I slunk right
down and sat on the floor, and just let the hot water
wash me away. It could have washed me right down the
drain for all I cared.

Made
me
disappear.

FOREVER

Later,
I think, *Enough's enough.*
Pull yourself together,
get dressed,
get some air.

I shove my hand in my coat pocket
and feel the crumpled note.

Fresh tears flood the corners of my eyes but

I'm not hiding.
I'm smoothing it out.

Bad news travels fast.
You never checked out Forever, did you?

It was signed,

Sorry he got you too,
Josie

LIGHTBULB

It was low, what he did, leading me on like that.
He meant something to me.
He had to pick up on that.
No *way* he didn't.
And for once, I thought I meant something
to somebody else.

Were those girls right?
Am I that stupid?

I thought Red Light was just a name he made up,
but after what they said, I thought I better look it up
and I went back inside. Turns out, it's a place in
Amsterdam for prostitutes. A whore sits in a
glass-front room with a red lightbulb. If the light's lit,
she's ready to do it. Men go to the red-light district

just to screw their stupid brains out.

I wanted to find the deepest, darkest hole there was
and climb in it when I read that. Here I was thinking
how great it was that we had our own secret place
with a nickname and all the time he really was calling
me a
whore.

Am I a whore because I like sex? Or because I did it
too soon? Or too much? Nobody ever calls boys
whores.

Why is that?

LONELY

I am way too young
to feel this used up.
This lonely.
I wish I was little again
and Mum
could make me some noodle soup
brush my hair
tuck me in
and tell me
everything is going to be
okay.

BEING HEARD

Mum walks in the door after work
and sees me slumped into the couch,
staring at nothing.
She's at my side in a second.

'Baby, what's the matter?'

I tell her,
not even trying to fight
this new round of tears.

She sits next to me,
wraps her arm around me,
rocking us gently back and forth
as I talk.

She hasn't done that
in a million years.

She's listening
hard.
Not yelling
or looking mad
or disappointed
or saying
I taught you better than that
or
how could you be so dumb.
Just rocking me
and listening
as I
spill
everything.

I finally stop.

She's quiet for another minute
or so,
like she doesn't want to interrupt
by asking
but wants to make sure I'm done
with my
emotional
heave.

Then she
smooths my hair
off my face
like she used to.

'What do you say we take tomorrow off?
A Mental Health Day. And we can talk,' she says.

'We could get our hair done
or do some shopping
or just take a drive along the coast,
how does that sound?'

I smile.
I nod.
I guess
for a while there
I forgot

I do
have a
friend
in this
world
after
all.

CRISS-CROSS

I'm what you call a Criss-Crosser.
That's a kid who doesn't belong to any one
group in particular,
but is by no means a loser.
I've got friends in pretty much all the cliques.
I criss-cross my way through the school.

I think it's because I'm pretty, but not cheerleader
pretty,
and smart, but not brainiac smart,
and artsy but not freak-show artsy.
I play the guitar,
which people think is pretty cool – as opposed to,
I don't know,
the bassoon or something,

which they'd probably think was geeky.

And I'm kind of funny, too.
My Dad likes to say I'm good at
finding the funny.

Anyway, somehow I get away with being
a Criss-Crosser.
And I get the feeling it's a hard thing to get away with
in high school,
even though I've been doing it all four years.

STILL

It's not a normal, everyday
occurrence
when one of the hottest jocks at PBH
asks me out.

I've certainly noticed him over the years,
I mean, who hasn't,
but I don't think he ever noticed me
until I saved his butt
in biology class last week.

We were cutting up dead frogs
and he didn't have the first clue what to do.
Some of the girls were going, 'Ooh, so disgusting,'

but I think it's pretty amazing to be able to peel back the skin of this
frog and actually see how all its insides work.

And I probably shouldn't admit this,
but even though that smell of formaldehyde
kind of smacks you in the face at first,
I kind of like how the sweet-and-sour smell grows on
    you,
sticking to the insides of your nostrils.
I bet years from now
I'll be able to close my eyes and still smell it.

So anyway, my frog was neatly
pinned to the pan
and I was just about to make a nice clean cut
with my scalpel
when he comes over to my lab station
looking like one of those stray dogs that
hang around the boathouse
looking for scraps.

'Hey, Aviva, how's it goin'?'

He knows my name?

'Fine, thanks. How's your frog coming along?'

'Not too good, actually.
I was wondering if you could help me out.
You seem to be sailing along,' he says,
just as I slice through the top layer of skin,
pull the veiny skin back, and reveal a perfect,
beautiful little froggie chest and abdomen.

'Cool,' he says.
'Way,' I say.

HIPPIE BY-PRODUCT

It's weird to call my parents hippies
since I don't really think there are actual hippies
any more,
but they are.

Dad's Birkenstock sandals
pre-date me,
and if I need money
for new jeans
you can bet I have to earn it
sorting the recycling
turning the compost heap
and packing a bag of canned nonperishables
for the Food Shelf.

It's no big shock, then,
that the dating situation is
pretty go-with-the-flow.
When my parents heard about the beach party,
it was just, 'Okay, honey.
Act responsibly. We trust you.'

And they should, actually.

PARTY

Amazing, amazing, amazing!
Did I say it was amazing?
Last night was *amazing*.
This crowd's music choices are, well *questionable*,
but they really know how to have fun.
And this boy,
I mean, I've dated boys before, but not like this one.
He lives for the rush of stuff like
sneaking his grounded friend out of the house,
driving too fast with the windows open, radio blaring,
turning off his headlights so it's like flying in midair,
crazy, daring, stupid, exciting stuff.

He has a way of sliding out of trouble,
plays the innocent really well.

Grown-ups seem to think he's such a good boy.
They are *so* wrong.

This boy gets any girl he wants.

Why does he want me?
From what I hear
he's been hanging out with a pretty wild girl
named Nicolette.

I'm not wild, but I am different.
Maybe that's why he wants me.
Maybe he's ready for something different.

MONDAY MORNING

'
Someone need rescuing?'

I can't get my locker open and here he is.
He didn't call me on Sunday, but here he is.

'Sure.'

He pops the lock and opens the door,
Mr Knight in Shining Armour.

'So, did you have fun at the party Saturday night?'
'Yeah, I did, thanks.'
'Y'know, I didn't get a kiss goodnight.'
'Yeah, tough break.'
'You're funny, I like that,' he says.

'Maybe if we go out again, I'll get another chance.'
'Maybe,' I say.

'So how 'bout it?'
'How about what?'

'You wanna go somewhere this weekend?'
'Okay, sure.'

He leans in to kiss me,
but I lean away,
a reflex response.

He grins.

'I'll call you.'
'Okay.'

SIGNALS

The buzz in the caf was that Nicolette
made a scene that morning.
It's all the jocks were talking about.
'Did you see her screaming? Man, she went off
on him,' one guy says.
'Dude, I'd hate to be him right now,' another says.

'Oh please, he already moved on to that Aviva chick.'

An alarm goes off in my head,
like the sound you hear on TV right before
a storm warning
flashes along the bottom of the screen,
but I shut it off.

'He moved on to that Aviva chick' is all I'm left with.

A LONG WEEK

I don't really get it, he came on so strong,
and now . . . what?

If this is his way of piquing my interest,
well,
unfortunately,
I guess it's kind of
working.

I *thought* he asked me out for this weekend, but
we don't have any plans yet
and it's Friday already.

Wait, here he comes with his friends.

'I'll call you, okay?' is all he says
as he walks past me and out of the school.

That's kind of rude.
What, does he think he's God's gift?
Am I just supposed to sit around and wait?
I've got a life.

Nicolette

FOREVER

I see Josie coming down Blue Hall.
She smiles and mouths the word
'for-ev-er'
to me on her way past.
That girl really has it together for a freshman.
For anyone. I mean, I'm older, but I'm sure as shit
not wiser.

Might as well just get it over with.

I take the book to a quiet corner of the library
where nobody is hanging out,
and open it to the back.

There's Josie's warning:

TO THE GIRLS OF POINT BEACH HIGH: BEWARE!!

There's a boy at this school who's only out for
one thing. . . .

Josie described him dead-on,
all except for the Terrible Lay part, sad but true,
he *so* proves the point of 'practice makes perfect',
from the looks of how many girls have
added major complaints about him to this book!
They took Josie's lead and ran with it.

I soak up every single word.
Then I add some stuff of my own.

I curl up in the corner
and start to read the actual book
from the beginning.

Might as well see what else there is
to learn
between the covers.

PRINCESS FAMILIAR

Saturday afternoon, I'm practising my guitar,
working on that song by
Alanis Morissette,
'Princess Familiar',
trying not to think about if I have a date tonight or not,
when the doorbell rings.

I get a knot in my stomach.

My father answers it.

'Aviva, you have a visitor.'

I don't want to be excited.
I want to be annoyed.

But here he is. On my doorstep. Smiling.
Mr I'm Too Sexy for My . . .

'Hey.'
'Hello,' I say, as casual as possible.

'Can I come in?'
I shrug.
'I guess so.'

'So, do you want to go out tonight?'

'Kind of short notice, don'tcha think?'

'Well, it just got thrown together at some guy's house
over by Gulf Pond. You know how these things are.
Do you want to go or not?'

'I don't know.'

'Oh come on, Viv, don't be like that,
what's the matter?'

'Nothing's the matter. I just don't like it
when people say
they're going to do something
and then they don't,
that's all.'

'I'm here now, aren't I?' He smiles that crocodile
smile.

'Yeah, you're here all right.'

'So, whaddya say?'

'Yeah, all *right*,' I say, trying my best to sound like
I'm doing him
a huge favour.
Does he even notice how annoyed I am?

'Cool, I'll pick you up at eight.'

Flash of white teeth and he's gone.

I hate being called Viv.

I pick up my guitar and go back to Alanis,
'Papa respect your princess . . .
she will find respectful princes familiar . . .'

And that last line of hers,
'please be,
just like my . . .'

and the song ends.

I just know she sings the word
'father'
to herself
every
single
time.

I know
I do.

MY DAD

' A party – tonight? Kind of last-minute, isn't it?
Is this the same boy you went out with last week?'

'Yes, Dad.'

'You know we trust you, honey. But it just seems to
me like he could have given you a bit more notice. A
little more *respectful* would be nice.'

And I hear Alanis croon.

THE KISS

The party is fun, your usual mix of the 'in' people,
dancing, listening to mainstream music,
drinking too much, being too loud.

I used to hear parties like this from my bedroom
window once in a while,
when they would spill out onto the street.

I remember one time last winter it was really cold, and
kids were running around outside screaming.
I thought it was so stupid they
thought that was fun.

Now I'm the one in the middle of the street,
a little high
way too loud,
yelling and laughing
and singing at the top of my lungs.

No doubt someone's peeked through window shades
to see what's going on out here
but it's just little old me
feeling free.
It *is* fun.

'I never did get that goodnight kiss last week.'
'Yeah, we've been over this.'

'How about now?'
'Is it time to say goodnight already?' I tease.

'Very funny, get over here.'

With one hand, he pulls me in to him.
With the other, he brushes the hair away from my face
and puts his mouth on mine.
We stay that way, in the corner of the yard,
my back against a stone-cold tree,
for quite a while.

All we did was kiss, but by the time we stopped
it felt like we had taken things pretty far, pretty fast.
And everything that was nagging at me melted away.

A SHORT WEEK

People always say
Time Flies When You're Having Fun.
It must be true, because this week really flew.

It's partially because I'm hyped up
from all this attention. It's not just
all the attention *he's* paying me either.
It's like suddenly I'm not just a
Criss-Crosser.
Suddenly I'm major Mainstream.
I never really thought I cared about that, and
I'm still not
sure I do,
but the perks aren't bad.

The cool kids saving you a seat at lunch,
being in on the weekend scene, stuff like that.

So now – another Saturday night, another party.

And WE are going.

POOL PARTY

What a scene!

Strictly A-list, something I've never made in my life.

I'm not exactly sure whose house this is,
but I've never seen anything like it.
It's near Point Lookout. Major bucks.
Huge, beautiful indoor pool. Changing rooms.
Very steamy. Very nice.
The only thing I would change is the music.
Really bad techno-pop crap.

I leave him for a few minutes to change
into my suit.
When I come back, he's talking

to a few of his friends. They're having a good laugh.
Then he waves and makes a beeline right for me.

I like that. The power of the string bikini.
Like white on rice. Stuck fast.
I laugh.

'What's so funny, gorgeous?'
'The look on your face, that's what!'

'Oh yeah, well, you won't be laughing for long!'

He pulls off his shirt, and pulls me into the pool
with him.

I come up for air, my wet hair flings around
slapping him in the face. We are still laughing.
I catch a quick glimpse of one of his boys giving him
the thumbs-up before I dunk him under the water.

TENSION

Some of my friends think I'm heading for trouble.
They say I don't hang out with them any more.
I guess that's true, but I'm a Criss-Crosser, I go
where I like.

Amanda, she's the most ticked off.
We've been friends since the fifth grade.
Amanda plays a mean French horn. And she's always
reading books by feminists like
Betty Friedan and Gloria Steinem.
I bet none of the jock crowd even knows
who they are.

Amanda and I were supposed to do something
over the weekend

and I kind of
forgot.
Saturday there was that pool party.
Sunday I watched the guys shoot hoops.

Monday morning
she's waiting by my locker.
'I never would have pegged you for a girl who
ditches her friends the second a hot guy comes along,'
Amanda says.
I'm *not* one of those girls.
But he *is* hot, and I love hanging out with him.

I guess I do sound like one of those girls.

Amanda and I make plans for next weekend.

YOU DON'T UNDERSTAND

Uh-oh.
There's Amanda by her locker in Orange Hall.
It hits me that the weekend came
and went
without her
again.

She's glaring at me.

'I'm really sorry, Amanda.'
'Forget it. You obviously had more important
things to do, I get it.'

'No, Amanda, that's not it. You don't understand.
When I'm with him, it's, it's,

I don't know,
like nothing else.
You don't know what he's like when we're alone.
He talks to me. He opens up.
He even told me about this girl Ashley
who kind of broke his heart.
You should have seen him, Amanda,
he can be so sweet and sensitive sometimes.
When it's just us.
He's so different from the guy you see with
his buddies –'

'*Aviva!*
Do you
hear
yourself?
Do you have any idea how many millions
of women
in the history of relationships
have spouted the
exact
same
crap?
He's *not* different. He's playing you.
And on the tiniest off-chance this guy really *is*
so different when it's
just the two of you,
why would you want to be with such a

screwed-up phony?'

'Amanda, I'm sorry to say this, but . . .
it just hasn't happened to you yet,
that's why you don't understand.
But I really am sorry about the weekend.'

'Save your sorries, Aviva.
Call me when you get your head out of the clouds.'

She slams her locker shut and leaves.

GROSS

We are walking down Yellow Hall after class,
his arm around my waist,
hand comfortably tucked into my back jean pocket.

'Did you know there's an old art-supply closet
at the end of this hall
that nobody uses any more?' he says.

'Yeah, except I heard some couple used it *plenty*.'

'What a good idea.' He grins at me.

'Oh right, how romantic. Forget it. Don't be gross.'

He drops it.

GLITCH?

We usually have plans together all the time these days.
I kind of count on it.
So when this Saturday came and went,
I wasn't sure what was going on.

I called him on Sunday but he wasn't home.
He still wasn't back
when I called him Sunday night.

There's that knot in my stomach.

MONDAY

'
Hey, beautiful, how's it going?'
He comes up behind me at my locker and kisses me
on the neck.

'Okay, I guess. Where have you been?'

'You remember, I told you I was going to hang out
with my brother for the weekend
up at UConn.'

He worships his older brother,
the BSOC (Big Stud on Campus).

Kristen, one of the jockettes,
gasps.

I don't look over, like it's no big deal.
Kristen's two lockers away.
She turns to the girl next to her and says,
not as quietly as I'm sure she means to,
'I wonder if he saw Ashley.'

Yes, *that* Ashley.
She goes to UConn now.

'No, you never told me you were going there.'
'Sure I did, Viv.'

'Do you know that I hate being called Viv?'

'Sorry. I had plans, *Aviva*.
You must have forgotten.'

'Whatever.'

'Let's do something after school.'
'All right,' I say.

My stomach unknots
a tiny bit,
even though he definitely didn't tell me
he would be busy.

I'm still picking up a Don't Get Too Comfortable vibe.

I try to push it out of my head,
along with thoughts of what he and the BSOC
might have spent all weekend
doing.

COURTYARD

Free period, so I grab my guitar from the music room
and head to the courtyard.

I'm sitting on one of the picnic tables,
playing and softly singing Joss Stone's
'Security',
when I see him out of the corner of my eye.

He's with one of his boys.
I don't think they think I notice them.

'Very cool. Very sexy,' I hear him say.

I tingle, like when my foot's asleep,

but all over.

'You got that right. You nail her yet?' his friend says.

I shudder.

'Shut up, man, she'll hear you.'
'Ooh, sor-ry, didn't know this one was different.'

There's that storm warning alarm again.

'Yeah, well, maybe she is, and maybe she isn't.'

My stomach doesn't quite know *what* to make of that.

SURPRISE

I'm in study hall.
The door opens.

He grins at me and slips the teacher a note.
Then he slides into the seat next to me and kisses me
on the cheek.

We study as close together as we can.
Every time he whispers
'You're so soft' or 'I want you'
in my ear I almost jump out of my clothes.
I'm having trouble controlling myself lately.
It's not like me.

NATURAL WOMAN

After study hall he walks me to my locker.
I never noticed how my jeans rub against my
thighs as I walk.
My shirt rubs against my chest too. Step, rub,
step, rub, making my
skin hot – on alert.
My face flushes like when I eat chilli peppers.
All he does is look at me, and I'm so, I don't know,
aware
of my body.

He puts his hand on that curve
right in the small of my back and I
twitch just a little.
He notices. Damn.

He smiles at me, sweet but crafty.
I feel so, so, so . . . charged up.
Energized.
Beautiful.
Just as the word enters my mind, he whispers,
'God, you're beautiful,' like he's in a church or
something.
A whole new surge of heat crackles through my body.

We stop at my locker and he puts his mouth on mine,
gentle and soft,
licks my lower lip with his tongue, not sloppy or gross,
just real light,
tugs on it with his teeth for a second.
I can barely stand.
He must sense me sinking into him, because I think
he's holding me up a little.

He's kissing me and kissing me and kissing me and on
the music sound track running through my mind,
Carole King is wailing, 'You make me feel like a
nat-ur-al wo-man,' and I sooo get why it's my mom's
favourite song.

I DON'T THINK

I can wait another nanosecond.
I'm dying for his body on mine.
I want him to smother me with his weight.
Breathe him in.
I'm ready.

He's coming over to study after school.
He can study me.
I take off my clothes in front of my mirror and look at
myself.
I'm tall, but not gangly tall.
Nice nose, a smile that's big and never fake.
I like my body, I like the curve of my belly.
I'm definitely not fat, and I'm not skinny, either.
I like my body, how cool is that?

I know plenty of girls whose bodies look like mine
and they think they're fat, when they're so not.
I wish they liked their bodies too.

I pull out a clip and my hair falls down.
It reaches the small of my back.
I've always loved my hair. It's brown, but not
mousey brown.
And it's wavy without being too curly or frizzy.
I move my head from side to side, letting my loose
hair tickle my skin.

I think I'll leave my necklace on – it's a silver figure of
Venus with her toes pointing downward, and she's
holding a sleek round garnet in her hands. It looks
sexy with nothing else on.

He'll be here any minute.
My parents won't be home until after dinner.
Perfect.

Joni Mitchell's *Court and Spark* keeps me company.
I play my guitar along with her.
Soothing sounds.

Doorbell rings.

Heart pounds.

I left the door open.
I hear his footsteps on the stairs.
'Viv?'
I still hate being called Viv, but not when it's him
saying it.

'Up here.'

He opens my bedroom door.

'Look at you.'

READY OR NOT

He walks over to the bed.
I am sitting on the edge,
completely naked
my guitar
strategically placed.

'Hi,' I whisper.

He sits down next to me,
doesn't say a word,
doesn't take his eyes off mine while he
gently takes my guitar away,
and lays me down.

He traces my lips with his fingers,

brushes the hair off my forehead.
Neither one of us is smiling,
I'm trembling and in that second I realize that
even though I'm dying for him, I'm scared, too.
I'm grateful that he hasn't started ripping off his
clothes or anything.
In fact, it's like the whole world
just went into slow motion,
like one of those old silent movies.

Joni Mitchell's words are coming out warbled and low,
her big toothy mouth opening and closing in my mind.

'It's okay,' I hear him say, as I fast-forward back
into the present.

He takes a condom out of his back pocket.
Is this really happening?
Why is he so prepared?
Does he always keep one in his pocket?
How many times has he done this?

Ugh, I'm killing my own mood.
I'm giving myself a stomachache.
I look into his eyes.

Oh God, is this really about to happen?

He smiles at me.

'You're sure you're ready?'

'Uh-huh,' I mumble, 'just kiss me.'

I don't want to talk, to think, to reason,

I've already made my decision.

'Please, just kiss me.'

FOREVER

His hands are big and they're everywhere,
stroking, squeezing
my body seems like one big blur,
I'm sure this is supposed to be making me hot and wild,
but I'm just feeling kind of groped.
Maybe this isn't all it's cracked up to be.
I guess I'm not participating all that much, because he
takes my hand
and puts it on his crotch.
I can feel him through his jeans.
I pull my hand back.

'What's the matter? Doesn't that feel good?' he says.
'Yes,' I manage to say, and let him put my hand back
where he wants it.

'Mmm,' he mumbles.
'You're so soft. You feel so good.'
Making him feel good makes me feel good.
I want more of that.

Pretty soon I have what I wanted.
The full weight of his body lying on top of mine.
Breathing him in.
This feels right.
His face presses into my neck, our bodies press
together,
in this split second it's like I've known him forever,
like we're connected, linked up.
I'll remember this feeling
forever.

Then he starts to move and I feel poked at again.
A mix of pain and pleasure
curls through my body.

The smell of him, the weight of him,
the sounds of him, all fill some kind of
ancient longing in me I never knew existed.

And then it is over.

Just like that.

Shouldn't an ancient void being filled
feel more profound?
I open my mouth and say the only words that seem
appropriate:
'I love you.'

But I don't think he hears me, because a minute later
he is snoring.

555-3142

He went home a little while ago.
He left his T-shirt here and his smell is all over it.
I keep taking deep sniffs. It smells so, so, so good.

I want to call him,
hear his voice.
Well, I want him to call me, actually.

But he isn't calling me.

I should just call him.

555-
No, I'll wait for him to call me.

The waiting is making me crazy.

555-31

NO.

Wait a minute, why should I have to wait for him
to call me? I'm not playing any games here.
If I want to call him, I'm going to call him!

555-314

555-3142 – quick, hang up!

Damn – he probably has caller ID so now he'll know
I called anyway.

I'll just call back and leave a message.
555-3142
'Hi, it's me. Give me a call when you get this.'

The phone doesn't ring.

DRIVE-BY

When my mum has to go out and do an errand later,
I ask if I can go.

I ask her to take a shortcut to the store that just
happens to cut down his street.

I slink down in my seat as we pass his driveway.

His bedroom light is on. I can see him working
at his desk.

He's home. He's just not calling.

THE NEXT DAY

When I get to school, I go by his locker.

'Hi, Viv,' he says.

I can't really get a read on him since he's being sort of friendly
but not normal. He doesn't kiss me hello.

'You never called me back last night.'

'Oh sorry, I got home too late. I went out with my parents,' he says.

'Oh.'

'I'll see you at lunch, okay?' he says.

'Okay.'

I walk away, nothing seems to be too wrong,
but nothing seems to be too right, either.
Did I do something?
Was I not really actually supposed to sleep
with him?

I want to throw up,
but I make it through my classes.
I wait for lunch.

LUNCH

There's a seat saved for me at his table, so it can't be
too bad.
He smiles at me a couple of times, but never really
looks at me or talks to me.
A canyon between us.

I look at Kristen.
I must look pretty bad, so she takes my arm and says,
'Come on, come with me.'

We walk to the bathrooms and I'm starting to shake.
'What's going on?' I start to cry.

'Don't cry, Viv, what happened between you two?'
I tell her a short version of yesterday.

'You told him you loved him?' she says. 'No wonder.'

'No wonder what?' I say. 'I don't even think
he heard me, he fell
asleep.'

'Oh, he definitely heard you. If he's acting weird like
this, he definitely heard you.'

'What, it's a sin to tell a guy how you feel?'
I'm really crying now.

'No, of course not, but you really should wait for him
to say it first,' she says.

'Why? That's so stupid! And I don't even know if I
meant it, it's just – how do you make love and then
not say 'I love you'?' I blubber.

'Sweetie, *we* call it making love, *they* don't,' she says.

The phrase 'nail her' flashes
like a huge neon sign in my brain.

I definitely think I'm going to throw up.

LAST WORDS

The last words he said to me when he was in my bed,
right before he left, were
'You're beautiful.
I'll call you tomorrow.'

He said he'd call me dozens of other times
and he usually did.
I kept going over and over those last words
to make sure I didn't leave anything out, or miss
some hidden meaning
that would have let me in on
what was going on now.

But I really don't have a clue.

THE TALK

Kristen arranged it. She says we should talk. I don't
know if he has anything to say. But I meet him after
school like she says.

He's waiting for me on our bench. I sit down
next to him. He's looking at his sneakers.

'What's going on?' I say.

'I don't know,' he says. 'Maybe things just got too
serious.'

'I don't understand. You were the one
who wanted
to sleep together.

You were the one
who wanted
things to get more serious.'

'But saying "I love you" is *too* serious, Viv,' he says.

'Stop calling me Viv!'

'Maybe we should just slow things down,' he says.

But I know he doesn't mean it.
Nobody ever
means
that.
A coward's way out.

I can't remember ever being this kind of seething mad
in my life.
Like I could smash him right in his
golden-boy face.

'You're a chickenshit coward,
you know that!' I yell.

'You push and you push, and tell me how beautiful I
am, and how special, and how much you want me,
and I finally serve myself to you on a goddamn silver
platter, and now you tell me you didn't really want to
get serious and that we should slow things down!

'God, you make me sick. My first time should have
been so great,
it shouldn't have been, it shouldn't have been . . .
Oh, get the hell away from me,
you make me sick.'

I am sobbing.

He just sits there.

I wish I could stop crying long enough
to quote some kick-ass lyrics.
Like Ani DiFranco. I hear her snarl in my head.
'Someday you might find you're starving,
and eating all of the words you said.'

But I can't get the words out between sobs.

'I'm sorry, Vi –
I mean, Aviva. I'm sorry.'

'Just go away.
God, just go away.'

I sit there, my nose and eyes running, big wet spots
seeping onto my sleeves. I sit there with my face in my
hands until I'm absolutely sure he's gone.

I don't ever want to see his face again.

What a coward.
What did I ever see in him?

THE MESSENGER

As if I'm not low enough,
Kristen comes up to me
in the caf.
I didn't go near the jock table today.
Found a different crowd.
Still, she finds me.

'Can we talk?' she asks.
'What about?'
'C'mon, Viv, you know what about, I'm trying to help.'

She sits down in unfamiliar territory. She doesn't care.
She has this air of entitlement about her.
Queen Bee can sit anywhere she wants
without worrying about disturbing the little people.

'He feels really bad, you know,' she says.
'Yeah, I'm sure he does.'
'No really, he didn't mean to hurt you.'

'Kristen, do you really think I'm that stupid? Of
course he meant to hurt me. If he knew everything
would be over as soon as we slept together, then he
had to know that would hurt me.'

'Boys like that don't think that way,' she says.

'Why, are *they*
that stupid?'

'Well, yeah, about stuff like this. They just don't
think that far ahead,' she says.

'Is that your way of defending him?
You want to be
next?'
A light dawns.

'Oh, you do, don't you? Well, don't let me stop you.
He's all yours,
just watch your back – and your heart,' I say.

'Now could you *please* leave and let me eat my lunch
in peace.'

'I tried,' Kristen says, shrugs her shoulders, as
Little Miss Perfect walks back to jock-land.

Oh *puh-leeze*, are we all so stupid? So blinded by a guy
who tells us everything we want to hear? Slobbers all
over us?

You *know* she's next.

He shoots me a sheepish look.
Coward boy needs a messenger girl.
Bad boy feels bad.
Too bad.
Too damn bad!

I'm such an idiot. And I'm so pissed at myself
because when I get older
and look back on my first time,
I was really hoping it would be a nice memory.

Too bad for me, too.

JOSIE

I'm still sitting in the caf,
not really sure what to do next,
when I notice this girl standing next to my table,
quietly waiting for me to notice her.

'Can I help you?' I say.
'No, but I'm hoping I can help you,' she says.

'What do you mean?'
'I'm Josie, I went out with him too.'

'Oh.'
'I think you should check out *Forever* at the library,'
she says.

'Forever?'
'Yeah, you know, the book by Judy Blume.'

'Why?'
'Because it wasn't your fault,' she says.

I try to say 'I know that,'
but I'm choking on my words through the tears.
She definitely hit a nerve.

She puts her hand on my shoulder.
Why is she being so sweet?
I don't even know her.

'Just do me a favour and check out *Forever*, okay?'
She takes her hand off my shoulder,
smiles,
and walks away.

I CAN'T BELIEVE

what I'm reading.

This poor book. Every little bit of free space –
in the back, in the front,
on the heading pages of new chapters,
even in the margins – there are things written
about him.
It's not good.

Josie's words have been embellished,
with a border and a label: FIRST ENTRY,
and an arrow pointing to her words.
This scribbler wants there to be no mistake:
Josie = Fearless Leader.

So many girls.

How could there have been so many girls
in four years?
I'm sure his buddies knew, but somehow he managed
to keep a low profile about it, and anyway,
who's got the time to keep up with
this guy's string of girlfriends?
Certainly not me.

I bet a lot of girls were mortified after
and just kept their mouths shut.
Does he even know the damage he has done?
I have to think he'd care, if he had a clue.
He's not a monster.
But then again, some of these girls sure think he is.

They've created their very own support group
within the pages of *Forever*.

The more I read, the more I realize
I'm not alone.
And it helps.
It really
helps.

WE THREE

I'm walking through Blue Hall
and I see Josie.

'Hey, Josie, thanks for the heads-up about
Forever. Very, um, informative.'

'No problem. Hey, Aviva, this is Nicolette,' she says.
'Um, hi. Wow. I guess I should say I'm sorry,' I say.

Nicolette looks at me
and says
nothing.

I open my mouth to add something,
anything,

but then Nicolette shrugs and says,
'I guess it's okay. You didn't know.
Right?'

'No, I *definitely* didn't know.
But I'm still sorry,' I say.

Just then, *he* walks by.

We all glare.

He had to expect at least some of us
would start comparing notes
sometime.

He puts his head down and hurries past.

We look at each other and
smile
a little.

MATERIAL GIRL

I never did write in the book.
I don't know why, maybe I'm saving up
to write a song about this whole mess.
Put a bad experience to some good use.
I never was one to buy into that whole
suffering artist thing,
but maybe there's something to it.

I do have a lot more . . . *material*
than I did before.

Maybe that whole hippie karmic cosmic
'everything happens for a reason' stuff
my parents spout
is true after all.

GIRLFRIENDS

Well, my head is *definitely* out of the clouds now.

I take my chances and look for Amanda at lunch
the next day.

'I heard what happened. You okay?' she asks.
Her question springs new tears to my eyes.

What a stand-up chick.
She doesn't have to be nice to me.
I don't deserve it.

'I will be, eventually, I guess.'
'Real convincing.' She laughs.
'Hey! Don't laugh at me.' I throw a French fry at her.

'You can keep crying, if you prefer.' She smiles at me.

'You pegged him right away, didn't you, Amanda.
You learn about boys like that
from all those books you read?'

'I'm sure my time will come.'

'Yeah, well, when it does, I'll be here.
Count on it.'

'I'm going to hold you to that.'

'You got it.' I start crying again.
'I'm so stupid.'

'You're *not* stupid. You know what, *Viiiv?*' She grins.
'You'll see the next one coming a mile away.'

Let's hope so.
I wouldn't want to go through this again.
But unfortunately, something tells me this stuff is
tricky.
I doubt this is the only mistake I'm going to make.
And I'm not so sure
it was a mistake, anyway.

I kind of hope he learns something too.

Even if it's only for the sake of the next girl
who comes along.
Or the one after that. Or maybe the one after that!

He's cute and all, but not what I'd call
a real quick study!

I laugh out loud.

And I'm happy for a second, because I still know how
to find the funny.

I like that about myself.

He told all his friends I was a PRUDE cause I wouldn't give him oral.

He told all his friends I was a SLUT because I would!

I HATE T.L.

Did you guys read that stuff about Pablo's party? I can't believe he made a BET on how many girls he could feel up?

Hey! Freak'n—>

I know, he wouldn't leave me alone until I let him prove it.

He got better, trust me!

Don't get me started, I've never been so mad in my life!

You are so not kidding! He cheated on me junior year and lied right to my face about it.

FIRST ENTRY

TO THE GIRLS OF POINT BEACH HIGH: BEWARE!!

There's a boy at this school who's only out for one thing.

I won't stoop to his level and call him by name but his initials are T. L.
(a.k.a. Two-faced Liar, Terrible Lay (I'm only guessing), Total Loser)
he's on the football and baseball teams and he never misses a party.

Sound familiar?   Yes   How lame

Don't go out with him!
(unless you want to use him for sex before he uses you)

Forewarned is Forearmed.   Good Idea!
Forever. YEAH!

How many times can I say I'm sorry. He really hurt me too, y'know.

I dated him when we were both freshmen and he was a terrible kisser!

OMG! Me four! Yuck!

Did he ever take anyone else to the Dugout?

ME   me 2
GROSS! Me three!

T.L.

you're better than that.

OK. What about the art supply closet? I know I went in there more than once.

Would that be a YES or NO?

I think I'm going to HURL!!

You guys shouldn't let a boy wreck your friendship.

I'm a senior. I went out with him Sophomore year. He made out with my ex best friend hurt me too when I was out of town.

There are plenty of nice guys at PBH. Nobody should date T.L. anymore!

HE BROKE MY HEART!

ACKNOWLEDGMENTS

Writing is a solitary experience. But if we're lucky, we have a community of people with whom we can share our journey. I consider myself exceptionally lucky in this area and am thankful for the generosity of so many people. Thank you, Beth Wright, YA librarian extraordinaire – you were one of my first invaluable readers and wisely suggested we send this book to Wendy Lamb. Hugs and thanks go to Jill Esbaum and her daughter Kerri (my first teen reader!), Erik Esckilsen (my first male reader!), Catherine Atkins, Stacy DeKeyser, Elizabeth Winthrop, Ellen Jackson, Laura Williams McCaffrey, Donna Freitas, Diane Davis, Jan Hughes, Lisa Angstman, Kristin Gehsmann, and Andrea White. Thanks also to Alex Flinn, Lara Zeises, and Cynthia Leitich Smith, who all offered wonderful advice when I needed it.

Love to Eileen Cowell (my sweet, forward-reading librarian mom). And props to the Kindling Words gang: I wrote many of these poems during one of our retreats, where it was suggested that my nascent short story was really the beginning of a novel (special shout-outs going to Karen Romano Young and Hope Anita Smith). *Gracias*, Karen Grencik, for your warm heart and your faith in my work. Thank you, Sarah Aronson, not only for your insights and enthusiasm, but also for your unwavering sisterhood. And big love and thanks to A. Harris Stone (for being the *best dad* a girl could have) and Laurie Foster (my fabulous, supportive sister).

And to you, Wendy Lamb and Alison Meyer, your confidence in me and excitement about this novel were thrilling. Alison, your talent for asking the right questions without looking for the "right" answers is incredibly impressive and unimaginably appreciated. And last, but most definitely never least, I thank my family for understanding my need for quiet writing time, and for their unconditional love and support. I love you all madly!